WE IMAGINE MUSIC SERIES
Vio's Violin

by Kenesha T. Ryce

Illustrations by
Kevin Jones

Copyright © 2018 Kenesha T. Ryce
Copyright © 2018 TEACH Services, Inc.
ISBN-13: 978-1-4796-0933-8 (Paperback)
ISBN-13: 978-1-4796-0934-5 (ePub)
Library of Congress Control No: 2018950325

TEACH Services, Inc.
P U B L I S H I N G
www.TEACHServices.com • (800) 367-1844

Imagine a book that allows a young violinist to hop inside their instrument and into a fairy tale land where musical questions are answered with a fun folk tale (and the real, technical answer—just to cover all the bases). "Why do I need to leave a space in between my hand and the violin in playing position?" Well, how else will the Peg family get through to visit their cousins in Tail Town? "Why can't I move my bow arm from my shoulder instead of from the elbow?" To keep the old man's house from falling down, of course!

These stories offer fun answers to technical, musical questions. Here, the young musician is allowed to travel into the world of music where the violin becomes the geographical landscape for fun stories that will help them remember and execute musical techniques.

"Stop Shaking My House!"

There was an old man who lived in a house.

Every so often, it would start to bounce.

The walls would jiggle, the floors would creak,

and after a while, the pipes would leak.

Now the old man found this to be quite peculiar,
And thought he should solve it in the near future.
He walked to the church. He climbed up the steeple.
He yelled to the ground to ask all the people.

He said, "Friends and neighbors, please listen to me.
I have a dilemma to present to thee.
My walls, they jiggle. My floors, they creak.
And would you believe it? My pipes even leak!"

His voice rang out all over the town.
After his speech, he climbed right down.
He felt quite discouraged. The townspeople looked bored.
The old man thought that he'd been completely ignored.

But a townsperson named Felix knew the criteria, To deal with the old man's urgent dilemma.
So he walked right up, sat the old man down, And told him the secret of the violinist who ran the town.

The secret he'd held onto for quite some time,
Was that the old man's house was built on a fault line.
The ground below his house would shake,
Because the violinist's bow was not moving straight!

The old man was only slightly disheartened,
For now he knew why his home had been such a bargain.
He asked, "How can I fix it? What can I do?
Where do I call? Whom can I sue?"

"The solution is temporary," Felix replied,
"But I have a good feeling it will suffice.
Here's the solution: With a loud shout,
You call to the violinist, **'STOP SHAKING MY HOUSE!'**"

"And that ought to fix it?" the old man asked with surprise.

"Yes, yes indeed," Felix replied.

The old man chuckled with great amusement,

Because his issue would soon be showing improvement.

Now, young violinist, it falls upon you, When the house starts to shake, you know just what to do. When the walls start to jiggle, and the floors start to creak, Just bend from the elbow and improve your technique!

So, how do you make sure your bow moves straight on the strings? Have a parent or teacher check to see if your bow is placed straight across the strings before you begin to play. Then, make sure to open and close your arm from your elbow instead of your shoulder. Remember, the old man's house is sitting on your elbow.

If you let your arm swing from your shoulder, his house will shake!

"The Day the Tunnel Closed"

Way up at the northern end of the fingerboard in Scroll City, lives the Peg family.

There's Papa Peg, whose name is Gee Peg; Mama Peg, whose name is Dee Peg; Brother Peg, whose name is Ace Peg; and little Baby Sister Peg, whose name is Eva Peg.

Every Sunday, Papa Gee, Mama Dee, Brother Ace, and Baby Eva hop in the car and drive through the tunnel, up the fingerboard, and over the bridge to Tail Town to visit their cousins, the Finetuners.

But one day, when the Pegs hopped into the car and tried to drive through the tunnel, it was closed, so they couldn't drive through the tunnel, up the fingerboard, and over the bridge to Tail Town to visit their cousins.

That made Papa Gee, Mama Dee, Brother Ace, and Baby Sister Eva very sad. Reluctantly, they turned the car around and headed back home to Scroll City.

When they got home, Papa Gee Peg called the tunnel operator's number. A person named Teacher answered the phone. Teacher said that the tunnel operator was too far away to reach by phone.

The tunnel operator's name was Vio Linist, and she sometimes fell asleep on top of the button that closes the tunnel. But if the Peg family got back into the car, drove back to the tunnel, and honked their car horn, they would be able to wake up Vio and get the tunnel to open.

Once again, the Peg family packed into their car and headed for the tunnel. When they arrived, Vio was still sleeping and the tunnel was still closed, so Papa Gee honked the horn, and Mama Dee, Brother Ace, and even Baby Sister Eva yelled as loudly as they could. This alarmed Vio, and she woke up with a start and quickly opened the tunnel to let the Pegs through.

Papa Gee, Mama Dee, Brother Ace, and Baby Sister Eva cheered as they drove through the tunnel, up the fingerboard, and safely over the bridge to visit their cousins, the Finetuners.

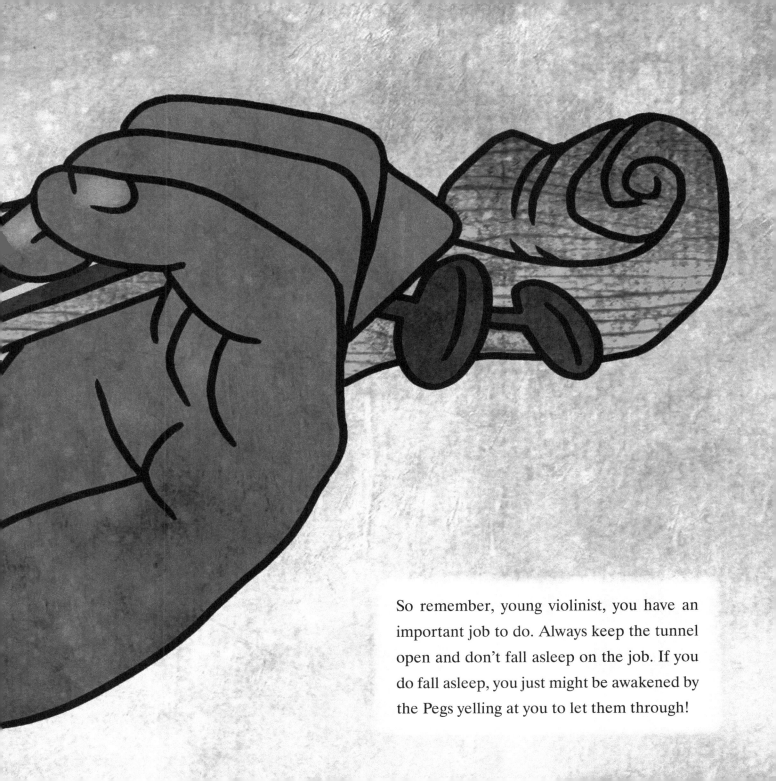

So remember, young violinist, you have an important job to do. Always keep the tunnel open and don't fall asleep on the job. If you do fall asleep, you just might be awakened by the Pegs yelling at you to let them through!

"Why must I keep space between my playing hand and the violin?" I'm sorry to admit that your pegs don't really need to travel to the tailpiece to meet their cousins. There are a few reasons why we always keep space in our hand while holding on to the fingerboard:

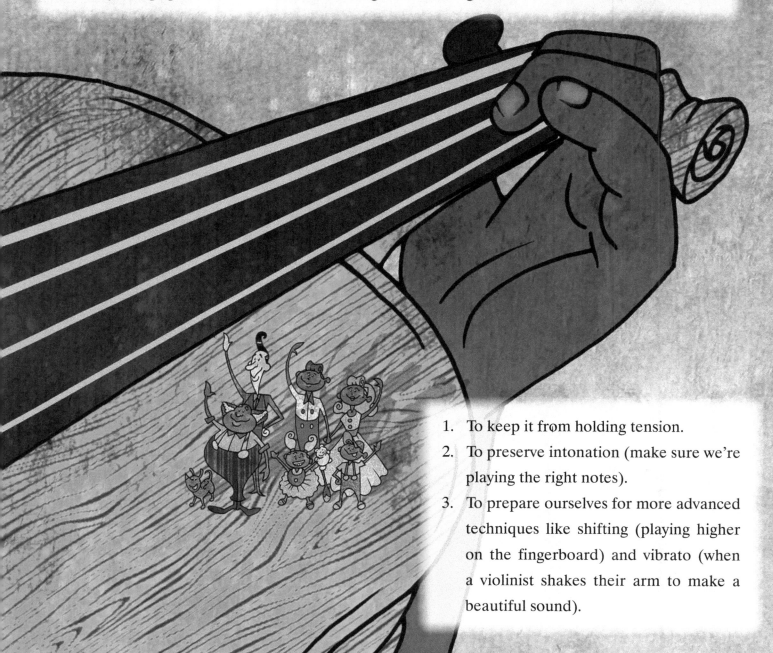

1. To keep it from holding tension.
2. To preserve intonation (make sure we're playing the right notes).
3. To prepare ourselves for more advanced techniques like shifting (playing higher on the fingerboard) and vibrato (when a violinist shakes their arm to make a beautiful sound).

I hope this little story helps you remember to keep the tunnel open while playing your violin because it will help you make more beautiful music now and in the future!

TEACH Services, Inc.
P U B L I S H I N G
www.TEACHServices.com ● (800) 367-1844

We invite you to view the complete
selection of titles we publish at:
www.TEACHServices.com

We encourage you to write us
with your thoughts about this,
or any other book we publish at:
info@TEACHServices.com

TEACH Services' titles may be purchased in
bulk quantities for educational, fund-raising,
business, or promotional use.
bulksales@TEACHServices.com

Finally, if you are interested in seeing
your own book in print, please contact us at:
publishing@TEACHServices.com
We are happy to review your manuscript at no charge.

CPSIA information can be obtained
at www.ICGtesting.com
Printed in the USA
BVHW021541230620
582135BV00005B/316

9 781479 609338